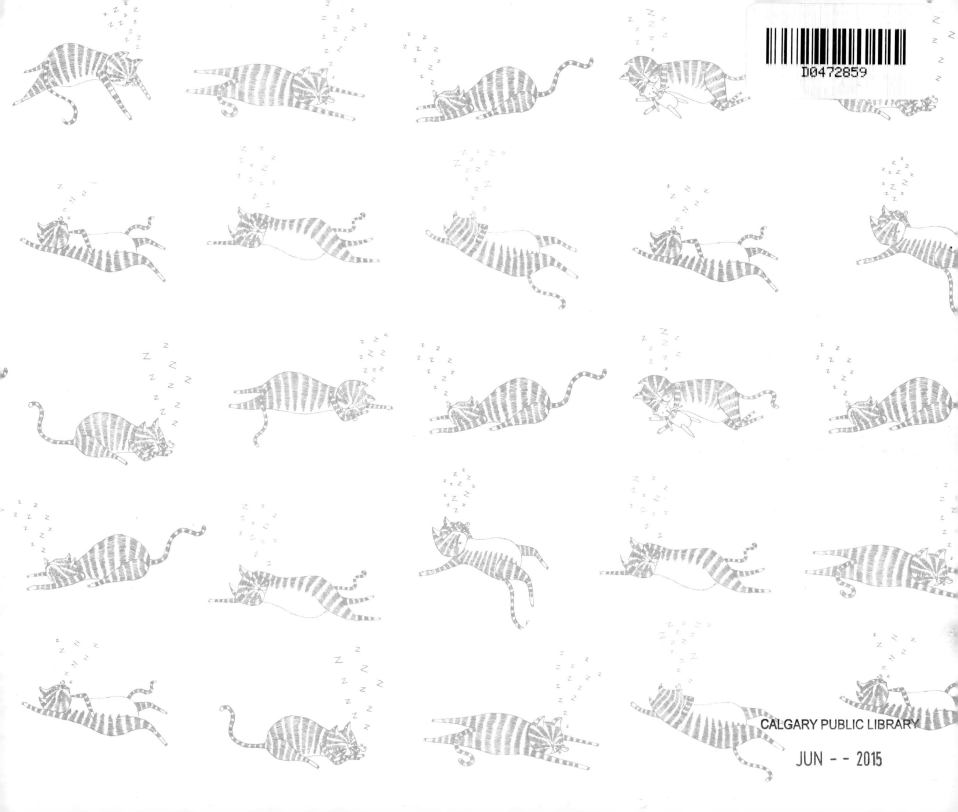

The AMAZING HAMWEENIE ESCAPES!

Patty Bowman

PHILOMEL BOOKS
An Imprint of Penguin Group (USA)

For my nana

PHILOMEL BOOKS

Published by the Penguin Group
Penguin Group (USA) LLC, 375 Hudson Street, New York, NY 10014

USA | Canada | UK | Ireland | Australia | New Zealand | India | South Africa | China
penguin.com A Penguin Random House Company

Library of Congress Cataloging-in-Publication Data
Bowman, Patty. The amazing Hamweenie escapes / Patty Bowman. pages cm
Summary: Hamweenie, the cat who is a legend in his own mind, escapes the clutches of the little girl who spoils him and makes his way to the circus, where he finds adoring fans that seem to be waiting for him. [1. Cats—Fiction. 2. Circus—Fiction. 3. Imagination—Fiction.] I. Title. PZ7.B6856Ane 2014 [E]—dc23 2013018196
Manufactured in China by South China Printing Co. Ltd.
ISBN 978-0-399-25689-9
1 3 5 7 9 10 8 6 4 2

Edited by Michael Green. Design by Siobhán Gallagher. Text set in 20-point Oneleigh.
The illustrations are rendered in pen and ink and
watercolors on watercolor paper.

Greetings, friends. Welcome to my prison.

I often imagine what life
would be like

beyond these walls . . .

. . . the fame, the adoration!

Unhand me, you hooligan! I will not tolerate such maltreatment.

To maintain a powerful physique, I abide by a strict diet.

What's this? At last . . . my stage awaits!

And now, without further ado, introducing the

extraordinary, the illustrious . . .

the Amazing Hamweenie!

I understand my charisma is overwhelming, but please, one at a time.

My autograph? It would be my pleasure.

Look at this mob!

I see they are expecting me.

It is obvious that I, the Amazing Hamweenie, am to be the star of the show.

I will give them a performance they will never forget.

Behold! The Amazing Hamweenie has arrived!

It seems my insane popularity has caused a stampede.

Listen here, monkeys, I'll let you ride my coattails to greatness!

Stop these shenanigans at once! This is no time for nonsense.

A wardrobe change?

Just in time!

I look amazing. As always.

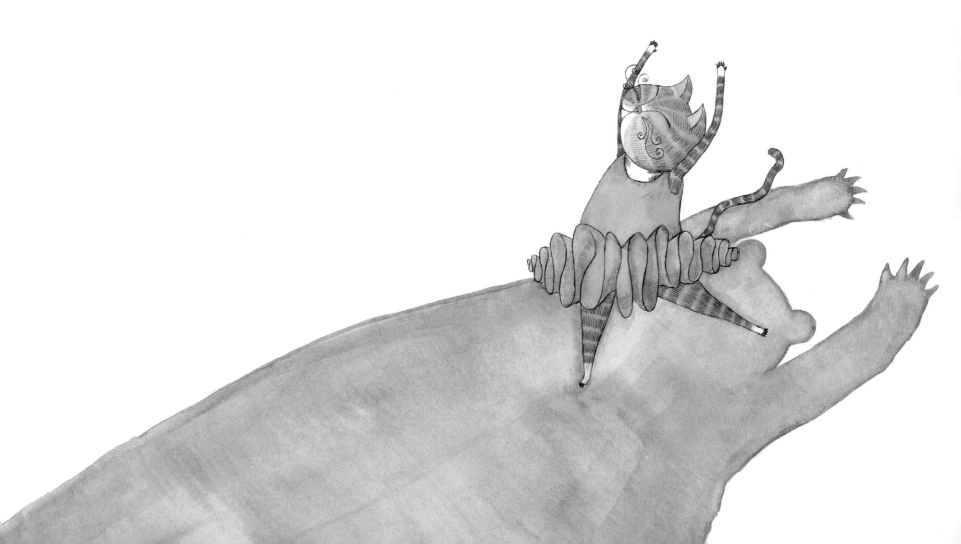

Who's this? An adoring fan?

How charming.

Salutations, feline brethren! Surely you recognize my greatness… Perhaps I've caught you at an inopportune time.

I need my beauty rest before my magnificent debut.

What's happening?!

Alas, foiled again.

Haven't you caused enough trouble for one day?

And now, without further ado . . . the Amazing Hamweenie!